My Little Thief

AUGUSTEN BURROUGHS   Illustrated by BONNIE LUI

Christy Ottaviano Books

LITTLE, BROWN AND COMPANY
New York   Boston

Chloe didn't like certain things, such as lightning storms, splinters, or bacon in cookies. She didn't much care for birds, either, especially the noisy ones in cages. Besides, you couldn't snuggle up with a bird, cage or no cage.

Once when she was in the car with her dad, she pointed out
the window to a straw man standing in the middle of a cornfield.
"What's that?"

"That's a scarecrow. To keep crows away from the crops.
Crows are a real nuisance out here in the country," he told her.
So crows were like bugs. Chloe liked bugs.

Chloe's mother had been pestering her to unpack the last few boxes. "Honey, we've been in this new house for almost a year. Why won't you finish unpacking?"

The truth was, Chloe liked those last few boxes stacked in her room. Partly because she'd forgotten what was inside them, and that was kind of exciting.

But mostly because at night in the darkness of her bedroom, the stack of boxes looked like the tower of a castle, and Chloe loved castles and planned one day to live in one.

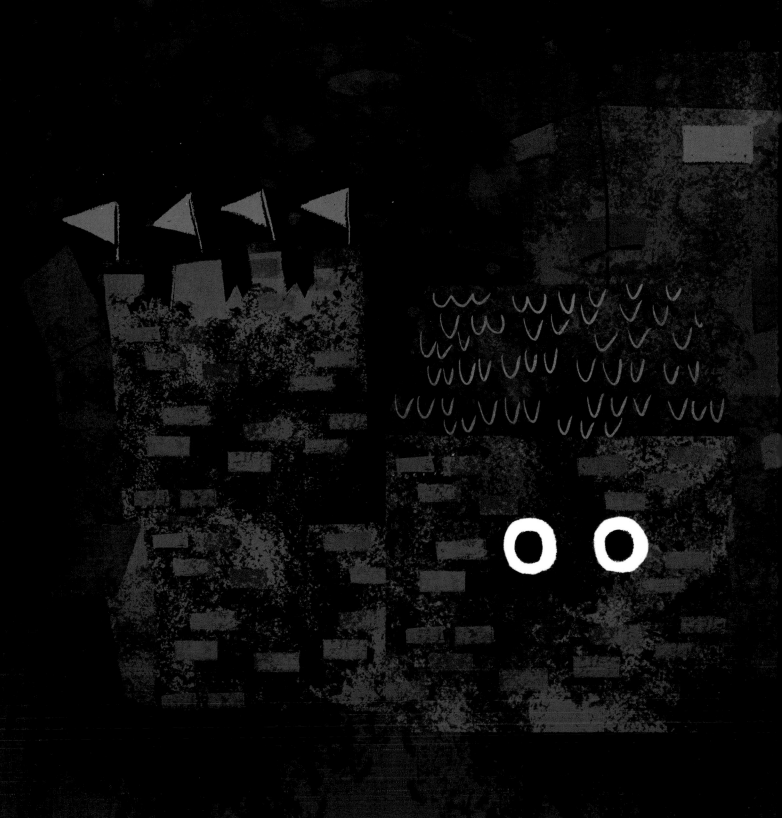

Also, she loved the dark. Lots of kids her age or even older were afraid of the dark. But Chloe found the dark to be a very friendly place where everything was wrapped in black, like a present.

Chloe also loved books, cupcakes, striped leggings, knitted stuff, anything with fringe, plus large floppy hats, pins, patches, shoes with different-colored laces, and broken or forgotten things. She liked her red hair and freckles, but not sunburn.

One afternoon, Chloe was sitting on her favorite rock in the backyard, nibbling a cucumber sandwich. She was reading about a shipwrecked family who is saved by monkeys when a crow swooped down and landed on a low branch nearby.

The crow cocked his head and stared at her. He seemed to be studying the button Chloe had pinned to her crocheted vest. The button was old and faded, with a picture of a rocket and the words "Girl Astronaut." Could the crow read? The bird peered deep into Chloe's eyes, then he looked at her sandwich and stomped one of his little feet.

This crow, so black and shiny he looked like glass, wanted her lunch. Chloe, who (as you know) didn't much care for birds, was suddenly intrigued. She broke off a crust and laid it at the farthest end of the branch. "There you go, Crow."

The crow strutted gingerly down the limb, glanced at Chloe, then snatched the bread and flew away.

The next day, Chloe returned to the rock with her book and a bag of popcorn. Just as she got to the chapter where a monkey teaches the dad how to lash the bamboo raft together, Crow darted down and perched on the very same branch, this time with something glinting in his beak. He hopped to the tip of the branch and released the sparkly object, which landed on a soft green patch of moss. It was a button that read "I'd Rather Be Fishing."

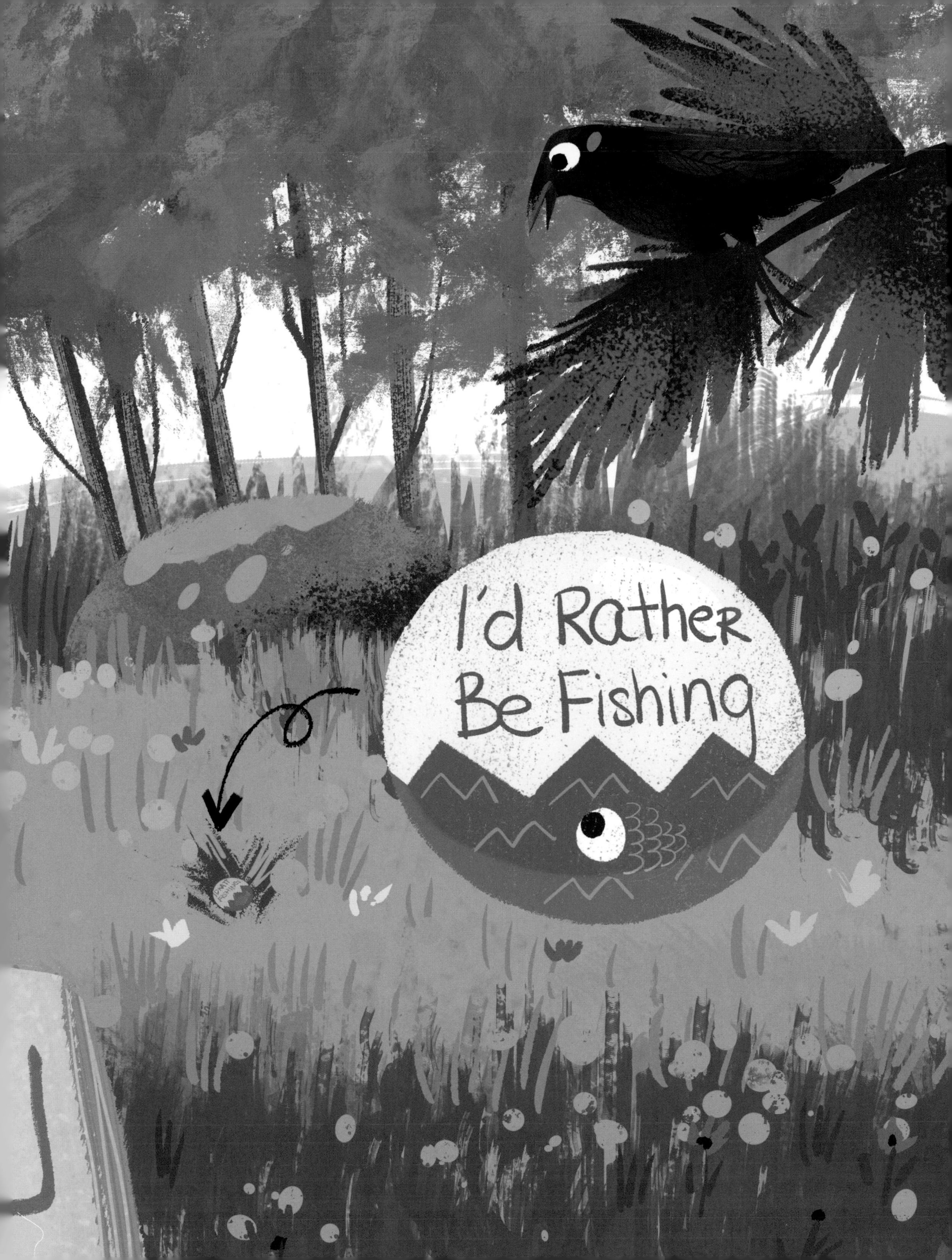
I'd Rather
Be Fishing

"Is this for me?" Chloe whispered, in awe. She removed her large straw hat and pinned the button to the band even though she wouldn't rather be fishing.

Crow nodded, looking pleased, then Chloe tossed a fistful of her popcorn onto the bed of moss. Crow cocked his head and examined the kernels. Then he fluttered down, quickly gobbled them up, and flew away.

Over the next few days, Crow brought Chloe many treasures:
a smooth shard of old pottery, a bottle cap, and a purple ribbon
just long enough to fit around her wrist like a friendship bracelet.

In exchange, Chloe offered Crow the top of a blueberry muffin,
three fresh green beans, a strawberry, and some scraps of yarn left
over from when her mom knitted her a scarf that was twice as long
as Chloe was tall. Maybe Crow could use it to decorate his nest.

When Crow gave her a single bright turquoise earring,
Chloe smiled wide and immediately pinned it to her vest.

But the next day at school, Olivia stopped Chloe and shouted, "You're wearing my grandma's turquoise earring. You're a thief!"

"I'm no thief," Chloe protested. "This was a gift."

"A gift? That's my grandma's earring that went missing yesterday after she placed it on the bathroom windowsill."

When math class was over, their teacher, Ms. Moldavite, asked each girl to tell her side of the story. To Chloe's horror, her teacher didn't believe her about Crow.

Ms. Moldavite made Chloe give the earring to Olivia. By the time she got home, Chloe was in tears.

After dinner, Chloe sat on the sofa between her parents. They had received a phone call from the school explaining what happened. "I want to believe you but it sounds far-fetched," her mother said.

Her dad nodded and scratched his chin. "Are you sure that wild imagination of yours has nothing to do with this? I mean, crows don't give presents to people—that's not a thing."

Chloe felt as if her parents didn't believe her. They thought she would steal. And then lie about it. Those were *two* really bad things.

Her mother sighed. "We'll talk more tomorrow. Time for bed." She glanced at her wrist, but there was no watch on it. "That's strange. Where did I put my watch?"

The next day, Chloe returned to her favorite rock. Crow was sitting on a rock nearby. "I got into trouble," Chloe told Crow. "Everybody thinks you aren't real and that I'm a thief." Just then, Crow dropped something onto the moss.

"You found my mother's watch!" Chloe gasped. "You didn't steal it,
did you?"

Chloe looked deep into Crow's eyes. She now realized exactly what
Crow was up to. He was "finding" objects and giving them as presents.
Crow was the actual thief even though his intentions were sweet.

A few minutes later, she opened the screen door. Her father and mother turned when Chloe cleared her throat.

Perched on her favorite purple knitted sweater was Crow, and from his beak dangled her mother's watch. Because Chloe was feeling betrayed by her parents, she addressed them formally: "Mother, Father, I'd like you to meet Crow." She looked at the black bird on her arm. "Crow, these are my parents. I think you found something my mother lost?"

Crow flew to the handle of the refrigerator, which startled Chloe's father. Crow leaned forward and was looking at Chloe's mother like, *Come on, lady, I don't have all day.* Chloe's mother carefully took her watch from Crow. "I'm so sorry, Chloe."

"We never should have doubted you," her father said. A crow that flies down from the sky and snatches up anything he likes and gives it to somebody as a gift? Who would ever believe such a thing? "Will you forgive us for not believing you?"

Chloe pulled off her hat, gathered her red, loopy curls that tumbled halfway down her back, and, in one motion, tied her hair into a stylish knot on top of her head. "I'm okay." She glanced at her dad, then her mom, and she smiled just a little. "But chocolate cake would take me from just okay to really, really good," Chloe said as she opened the screen door so Crow could fly home.

Chloe would try to explain to Crow that stealing wasn't the same as finding. And that stealing was bad. But rusty old bottle caps and scraps of purple ribbon were the best! And he didn't need to bring her anything anyway because the real gift he had given her was himself: He was her friend. And Chloe was his friend.

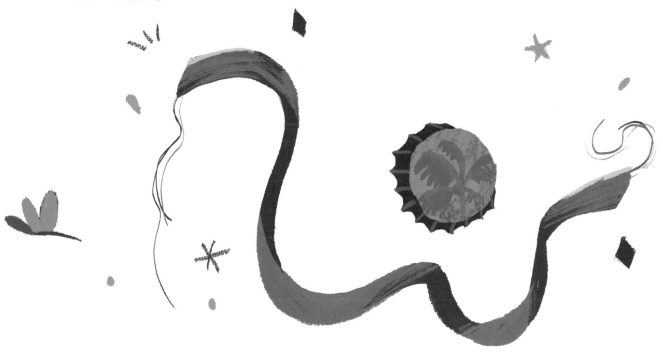

And maybe the day after tomorrow, she could introduce Crow to Olivia and everyone else at school so that they would know she wasn't a thief, she was only good friends with one. Imagine if she and Olivia actually ended up being friends.

Also, tomorrow she would bring Crow macadamia nuts, because they came from Hawaii, which was practically on the other side of the whole entire world, and she was pretty sure Crow had never tasted anything from so far away.

Christopher Schelling

A NOTE FROM THE AUTHOR

A number of years ago, I read a news story about a girl who made friends with a crow. Every morning she filled the birdbath with fresh water and left nuts nearby for a treat. In return for her kindness, the crow brought presents for the girl: small, rusty bits of things—buttons, screws, and other shiny treasures. I loved this story so much I couldn't stop thinking about it. What a thoughtful, considerate girl. And what a thoughtful, considerate crow—a little thief with a heart of gold.

To all the friends we make in nature —BL

ABOUT THIS BOOK

The illustrations for this book were done in mixed media. This book was edited by Christy Ottaviano and designed by Tracy Shaw. The production was supervised by Nyamekye Waliyaya, and the production editor was Jen Graham. The text was set in Patrick Hand, and the display type was hand lettered by Kelly Anne Dalton.